Worry with Mother

Worry with Mother

101 Neuroses for the Modern Mama

Francesca Hornak
with illustrations by Dorrance

PORTICO

First published in the United Kingdom in 2016 by
Portico
1 Gower Street
London
WC1E 6HD

An imprint of Pavilion Books Company Ltd

ISBN 978-1-91023-235-4

A CIP catalogue record for this book is available from the British Library.

10 9 8 7 6 5 4 3 2 1

Reproduction by Mission Productions Ltd, Hong Kong
Printed and bound by Times Offset (M) Sdn Bhd, Malaysia

This book can be ordered direct from the publisher at www.pavilionbooks.com

Contents

Are you sitting comfortably?
Then I'll begin.

For the first few months of my son's life, like any dutiful new mother, I referred constantly to parenting books, websites and magazines. I was in thrall to Britain's two biggest baby gurus, Gina Ford and Penelope Leach, whose books I had been lent by a friend. But Gina and Penelope were a terrible combination, because they had opposing theories on everything. Gina (a routine fanatic) made you feel disorganised, and weak-willed. Penelope (the original earth mother) made you feel heartless for ever putting your child down. For each problem I faced, there seemed to be two completely contradictory solutions. Every time I looked up one anxiety, I came away with five new ones.

Then there were the worries that I conjured out of thin air, which seemed rational at 3am, but sounded ridiculous at the GP's surgery. Whenever I shared these fears with other

parents, though, I found I was not alone. Most mothers, it transpired, know the 3am panic. My personal low point was the time my son's nanny (who I was able to semi-spy on) changed his morning's itinerary, by taking him to the library without telling me. I worked myself up into a private frenzy, imagining what else — besides illicit library visits — she might be concealing. Then there was the time I read, in tiny print, 'Not Suitable For Infants' on a packet of flaxseed I had been sprinkling on his porridge, having read it was a good source of Omega 3. I spent a feverish night researching 'flaxseed overdose', and kicking myself for not giving him Weetabix, like a normal person.

This was the start of *Worry With Mother*, which I hope captures some of the madness of modern mothering. Of course, maternal anxiety is nothing new. It's just that mothers today are bombarded with more tips, advice, goals and checklists than ever before. This is why I left the worries in this book hanging, unanswered, because the essence of maternal fretting is that you can't win. Besides, the one thing the world doesn't need is more parenting advice. Personally, I take greater comfort in discovering that someone else is as neurotic as you. This is where Google is invaluable. To find you aren't the first mother to wonder: 'Can toddlers digest sweetcorn?' and then read a whole thread by people who seem even crazier than you, is far more reassuring (and entertaining) than Penelope or Gina.

Luckily, the friend who had lent me the books got pregnant again, and I was able to get them out of the house for good.

Feeding

If I breastfeed on demand, will my baby become a comfort eater in later life? Then again, if I bottle feed, will we fail to bond? What if we have a formal, strained relationship forever, culminating in a huge row in 30 years and me not being invited to her wedding?

Why does everybody seem to think they have a 'hungry baby'? How hungry must they appear before they are classed as medically hungry? On this note, why can't anyone agree when to start solids?

I have just made a roux for my toddler, a requirement of Annabel Karmel's Mini Fish Pies. I wouldn't dream of making a roux for my husband. What does this say about our marriage?

I know French children don't throw food. What I need to know is, how can I behave more like a French grown-up, in order to achieve this? Would it help if the whole family dressed in Petit Bateau? Except my children throw so much food, I'd spend my life at the drycleaners.

Does pesto (Waitrose fresh, not jar) count as one of my fussy eater's five a day?

I think my child has an intolerance to sliced bread. He has no symptoms with pitta, or Cranks. Is this a recognised allergy? Is it my fault for eating so much Hovis while pregnant? Can I let his school know that he can't tolerate 'supermarket loaves'?

Will other mothers judge me for putting juice in my ten-year-old's lunchbox? If I forbid juice, does that make me mean and neurotic? I thought coconut water was okay. But when I tried this, my son spat it at me. Now I'm concerned he's 'on the spectrum'.

I want to show my teenage daughter I am 'laid back' about diet and body image. But I don't want to put on weight by casually eating loads of carbs in front of her. Hmmm.

How can I ensure my son eats vegetables on his gap year, teaching in Peru? (But not raw ones, covered in E. coli-infected water... Or is it E. boli?). Should I write to his host mother, to explain that he needs vegetables to be hidden in sauces? Would that be weird? How else can I prevent him developing scurvy?

What, exactly, is in the giant tub of protein powder my 30-year-old son keeps in our cupboard? I worry it may be a cover for steroid use, or contain cocaine or something terrifying. I am racked with guilt that he thinks he needs to 'bulk up'. I must have started him too late on solids as a baby.

Playtime

How many hours a day must I sing 'Old Macdonald' to my newborn, to qualify as a good mother?

I bought a large playpen, and filled it with developmental, wooden toys. But unless I get into it with my nine-month-old daughter, she hangs off the gate and roars. She looks like a caged animal, and it takes up half our sitting room. But without it, she fingers the plug sockets. What to do?

My son goes weirdly listless and vacant in our Rhyme Time class. I keep trying to bounce him more vigorously and sing 'Row Row Row

The Boat' more excitingly,
and he just gazes into space.
I'm worried everyone else
will think he has
a low IQ.

When other mothers say
'play date', I want to vomit.
This is hampering my
toddler's social life.

I can't get the Peppa Pig
theme tune out of my head. It
has become like an intrusive
thought. My husband told me
I was moaning it in my sleep.
Am I having some sort of
breakdown?

Imagine if my twins were playing, and one got into the chest freezer, and the other shut the lid and then couldn't open it, and the first twin got hypothermia?

We have a bubble gun at home,
which I insisted my husband
call a 'bubble hairdryer', so as
not to promote violence.
He refused, and even said he'd
rather his sons got
into guns than hairdryers.
Now I'm afraid I have a
homophobic husband, and that
my babies will get into a gang
as teenagers.

My eight-year-old daughter
has been invited to a makeover
party. Should I decline
the invitation, on gender
stereotyping grounds?

What is Game Of Thrones?
Presumably not musical chairs.

My husband and I are away for the weekend. What if our children decide to have a party, which they advertise on Facebook, only for it to be gate-crashed by 400

youths who trash our house, overdose on 'legal highs' and finally stab each other, as so often happens in the *Daily Mail*?

Developmental Milestones

Why won't my newborn look me in the eye? He always seems to be looking past me, into the middle distance. Could he have empathy issues?

My son can't walk, at 17 months. I've started telling people he is only 13 months, to buy more time, but as he is quite chubby they always look shocked and say, 'Ooh, big boy, isn't he!' I'm not sure if I'd rather they thought he was obese, or failing to meet milestones.

My daughter said her first word, 'Tesco'. I'm dismayed that she went for such a horrible brand, especially since we only go there in emergencies and try to patronise local shops. Why couldn't she have said 'Mama'?

I hate Gina Ford's *My Contented Baby's Record Book.* I was meant to write everything in it, but over three years all I entered was my son's birth weight, and that he liked bananas. Now it just sits on the shelf, reminding me how useless I am, and how I failed to cut a lock of his newborn hair.

My four-year-old is frighteningly advanced. Yesterday I found her reading the *FT*. Now I'm afraid she won't be able to relate to her peers. She will be the

over-chatty child at the end of the crocodile on school trips, holding hands with a parent because she prefers adult company.

My daughter's teacher pointed
out that she struggles to hop,
and suggested I take her to
the GP. At the doctor's she
hopped fine, which made me
look silly, but then drew a
gruesome picture of people
drowning, while he talked.
Now he has referred me to a
child psychologist, in light of
the drawing. Why did I listen
to the teacher?

My child keeps putting on a very irritating Scottish accent. When I told him to stop, my psychologist friend said he was 'experimenting with silliness' and I must not suppress this developmental stage. How long will it go on?

I took my 12-year-old to buy her first bra. She wanted a black lacy one, with matching pants that said: 'If you're rich, I'm single.' I wouldn't buy them, but when I told my friend she hinted that I was inhibiting her nascent sexuality and might give her a shame complex.

I have just seen my son's first
pubes, around the plughole.
This is the end of an era.
I feel like something dark has
entered the home.

My daughter has had her heart broken, for the first time. Conscious that this was a big deal, I suggested we watch romcoms and eat ice cream, like mothers and daughters do on TV. She looked repulsed and said I was 'basic'. What does this mean? Why can't I ever do the right thing?

Health & Safety

If I use self-tan while pregnant, will it leach into my womb and turn the foetus orange – causing a misdiagnosis of jaundice? Would it be OK if I just tanned my legs, arms and head, and left my bump white?

I keep waking my newborn up from perfectly good naps, convinced she has stopped breathing. I've taken to holding a mirror up to her mouth, to check for her breath. I thought this ingenious, but my sister told me I was 'on the edge'.

I decided to hang a Christmas decoration over my son's changing mat, so he would have something stimulating to look at. But I didn't secure it properly, and it fell on his face. He screamed so much I am worried I have done him some awful damage, even though it was only a small plastic snowman. I have been lying down, dropping it on my face from a similar height to test how much it may have hurt – but I can't recreate the shock he must have experienced. I think I might cry.

When can I stop sterilising everything that goes in my baby's mouth? The other day I turned round and he was licking a public loo seat. But I can't shake my fear of unsterilised bottles, after reading that bacteria in milk may 'colonise the teat'. Why did they have to put it like that?

The only way I can get my daughter to sleep is by pushing her in the buggy, quite forcefully, back and forth over a particular patch of cobbles near our house. She seems to find this relaxing. But one day I suddenly thought, did this amount to shaking her? I haven't been able to sleep since (nor has she).

I'm anxious about the similarity between blueberries and deadly poisonous ivy berries. We don't have ivy berries growing in our garden, but my children could easily encounter them in a park. Should I ban blueberries from the house, to prevent any confusion? The tricky thing is, they are a super-food.

I have become obsessed with the idea of urban foxes, since reading a news story about a coyote in Minnesota that built a den under a child's bed, and bit it during the night. Is this a legitimate anxiety in Brighton? We do have foxes.

My son is about to start 'big school'. He will be taking the train alone for the first time and, since he is very slim, I'm terrified that he will fall down the gap between the train and the platform. I suggested he go to a different school, near a station with a smaller gap, but my husband won't agree as it got a low OFSTED rating.

THE GAP

I don't want my teenage daughter to know I wait up for her when she goes out, so I usually hide in the car with a thermos of tea, and creep in once she's back. Last night I came in too soon, and she was in the kitchen eating a kebab. I told her I had been gardening, as I couldn't sleep, but she looked doubtful. Should I confess, and reveal I don't trust her, or let her think I am leading a double life?

My 19-year-old son is going to Thailand, for something called a Full Moon Party. He has never shown an interest in nature before, so I'm keen to encourage this. But I'm told these parties can get quite wild. Can I stand two weeks of wondering if he has been kidnapped by pirates?

Technology

Is it wrong to Photoshop my newborn's flaky scalp before putting pictures on Instagram?

I've got into a habit of watching *Real Housewives of Atlanta* while breastfeeding. Could it be seeping into my baby's subconscious? If one day she gets a boob job and marries a rich, bullying brute, it will all be my fault.

My toddler treats any flat object (books, DVD cases, chopping boards) as a pretend iPhone, swiping, 'texting' and

talking into them. Is this a giveaway that I let him play with my phone all the time? I know this breaks multiple good mother rules.

Which idiot decided that
battery-operated toys should
require a screwdriver, and 20
minutes of hands-free time, to
get them started again?

My eight-year-old daughter spends hours looking at incredibly boring 'vlogs'. She insists on wearing headphones, so I can't hear them. The other day I looked at my laptop history, and found she'd been watching a middle-aged Minecraft fan talking about taking his dog to the vet. Why would she watch this? What about Zoella?

Is a selfie stick the thin end of the wedge? Did I really just say 'the thin end of the wedge'? I'm turning into my mother.

My son has banned me from friending him on Facebook, as he says I will stalk him. I got round it by having a profile as the family cat, which is the only basis on which he'll accept me. Then I discovered he has two Facebook accounts, one innocuous, and another I don't know about (full of drugs and orgies, no doubt).
I can't keep up.

I keep facetiming my daughter's boyfriend by accident. I think he thinks I fancy him. To make it worse, I'm always looking especially rough when I do it.

Why must my children document every moment of their existence online? What if some thoughtless tweet goes viral, and ruins their lives? Also, I'd like to be able to eat out without waiting for them to photograph everybody's food. It's like dining with forensic detectives.

My 31-year-old son is still living at home. I know this isn't good, and that I should encourage him to move out. The thing is, I rely on him to operate the TV, my laptop and the central heating timer.

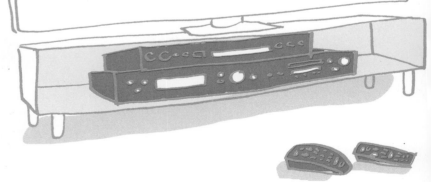

Education

What To Expect When You're Expecting suggests my husband and I play the bump our favourite songs. My husband is a nu-metal fan. Is this still OK?

Yesterday, my one-year-old came home from nursery with teeth marks on her leg. Could I request to see her classmates' dental records, to ascertain the biter? I feel his or her mother should know.

My husband and I have been going to church, to secure a place for our toddler at a Catholic pre-school. The problem is, I've become inconveniently

God-fearing. After listening to all the sermons, I'm not sure my conscience can stand taking a place from a truly Christian child.

My two-year-old son has shown an early aptitude for the violin, but the Suzuki method doesn't start until three. What to do?

I think my daughter's tutor partner is holding her back. Can I sack the other child?

I thought I was meant to take my children to lots of extra activities. So I booked drama, French, dance, tennis, swimming, coding, extra maths, judo, fencing and gym. Now I've read that I am 'raising their cortisol levels to those experienced by CEOs'. If I don't drive them to all these classes, though, they will just stare at their iPads, grunting.

I tried to do my ten-year-old's sample SATS paper, and got 17 out of 40. Does this constitute a problem?

At parents evening, my son's art teacher produced some still-lifes of biscuits, that were far too good to have been by him. She was so full of praise that I said nothing – despite being cross with the school for hiring such useless teachers. Am I a bad person?

My daughter and I had a row after I said, 'Do your best, we love you whatever grade you get,' when she left for her first A-level. I was trying to show unconditional love, but apparently it was patronising.

Last year I said, 'I know you'll do brilliantly,' and she complained I was putting her under extra pressure. Before that, I said 'Exams don't matter,' and she asked why I looked at league tables. I can't win.

My daughter
is taking
pole dancing
classes, while
at university.
She says it is
'empowering'.
This wasn't
how I envisaged
her time at
Cambridge.

Other
Parents

I have nothing in common with my NCT group, apart from having given birth at the same time. I'm running out of excuses to avoid their four-hour coffee mornings. Why did I pay for friends I don't want?

I've noticed that when other mothers return to work, they joke about the joy of going to the loo alone. I didn't realise I was meant to take my baby into the loo with me – I always left him in his Moses basket. Could I have given him a complex by depriving him of loo-time?

A very earnest single dad keeps chatting to me, in the sandpit. I dread him appearing, but my daughter has taken a shine

to his little boy. The dad is now trying to set up a date for our children. Why do I feel like I'm having an affair?

I thought fairy cakes would be safe for the school bake sale, but everyone else made gluten-free cookies, or cakes with vegetables in. Nobody bought mine, which were iced bright green and decorated with hundreds and thousands. Now I feel six years old again, myself.

I left my son with my 80-year-old mother-in-law, for the weekend. She told me that she'd let him stay up to watch 'Gay Rabbit' on TV, which she assumed was a quaint children's programme (she wasn't wearing her glasses). How can I explain that it's a porn channel?

For World Book Day, another mum and I made a pact we would both send our daughters as Roald Dahl's Matilda, since they would only need to wear school uniform. On the day, she sent her daughter as the BFG, with stilts, prosthetic ears and a hand-knitted Snozzcumber. I found this deeply disloyal, but when I broached it she said, 'But it's all Dahl!' I hate her.

I have become strangely obsessed with a Californian mother at my son's school, who always looks perfect and wears yoga gear at all times. I keep stalking her on Instagram, and am dying to see her house. Unfortunately, our sons have no interest in each other. How can I get them to be friends, so I can hang out with his mother?

I grounded my daughter after she and a friend got very drunk on tequila. Her friend's father approached the issue by taking his daughter to a wine tasting, so she'd learn to 'treat alcohol with respect.' Apparently, I have made it the forbidden fruit, which is disastrous with teens. I thought I was meant to be 'a parent, not a friend.'

My son is marrying a very nice girl, but her parents are a bit UKIP. They have insisted on Union Jack bunting in the marquee, and I'm dreading the father-of-the-bride speech. Could I sabotage the mic?

While babysitting for my daughter, I was meant to defrost the stewing steak in the freezer. I accidentally defrosted her placenta, instead. She'd been keeping it to bury at my grandson's 'naming ceremony', and was furious with me. Why can't modern parents just have christenings?

Behaviour and Boundaries

As part of baby-led weaning, I've read that infants must 'explore' their food. My daughter eats yoghurt with her fingers, and likes to put carrot sticks in her nostrils. My mother-in-law always says: 'Don't play with your food, darling.' How can I explain that she is not playing, but exploring, and that this is to be encouraged?

My one-year-old son can only get to sleep if I let him tweak my nipples. I know this is not a good habit to encourage, but this is outweighed by my need for sleep.

My child won't share. I keep saying: 'Why don't you give someone else a turn?' but she just shouts 'MINE'. Yesterday, on the bus, she snatched Sophie-The-Giraffe out of a baby's mouth. Should I have another child, so I can blame her whims on jealousy?

While I was paying for petrol,
my three-year-old stole a pint
of milk from the garage.
Is this an early indicator of a
criminal mind?

I forgot I'd put my son on 'time out' on the naughty step, and left him there for an hour, as I was distracted by an email upstairs. How can I preach about good behaviour, when I'm such a bad mother?

I would like to practise Free Range Parenting, as it sounds wholesome and outdoorsy. But my children just want to watch Netflix. How can I get them to range, freely? Also – can I fit them with a chip, so I know where they are, and can make sure they're avoiding roads?

Most evenings, my son texts from his bedroom, asking what's for dinner. He only comes down if he likes what I'm cooking. My sister was shocked by this, and said it 'explained a lot'. What did she mean? I've read that you're supposed to offer children choices.

I thought teenagers were meant to 'push boundaries'. But my daughter and her friends show no interest in smoking, drinking or underage sex. They spend the whole time online, instead. What's wrong with them? This is making me feel like Eddy, in Ab Fab.

My son kept stealing teaspoons, and I became convinced he was a heroin addict. But when we confronted him, it turned out to be part of a sculpture for his AS-level Art, titled 'Generation Spoon-Fed.' I feel faintly implicated in the title, and irritated, as they were a wedding present.

How long can I blame all bad behaviour on teething, growth spurts or hormones?

Relationship-Building

I'm confused by attachment theory. My one-year-old daughter seems indifferent to my return from the office. Does this mean her attachment is 'secure', or that she has no attachment to me whatsoever?

My three-year-old daughter
has an imaginary friend called
Neil. I asked her what he was
like and she said he was 'like
Father Christmas'. Should
I be concerned?

Interviewing nannies, I have discovered that my sons are very superficial. They only like blonde candidates, particularly one who looked like Gisele. She was brilliant with them, but I don't know if I can bear having her around the house. Also, how did I breed tiny chauvinists?

Having had no friends, my son now has one silent friend. The other day I found them beating teddies with the pepper grinder. This isn't how I'd envisaged his inaugural play date. But is one strange friend better than no friends?

My seven-year-old daughter calls my husband Chris. I can't explain why this depresses me. Why won't she call him Daddy? Is this the start of a lifelong difficulty forming intimate relationships with men?

How can I police my son's contact with Internet pornography? Will it give him a warped view of sex? I've been growing my armpit hair, so he doesn't grow up believing women are hairless, but he seems oblivious. It's a bit sweaty. Can I stop?

I know my 12-year-old daughter must have the HPV jab. I just don't want to think of my baby as a sexual being. Couldn't they call it something else? The jolly jab, perhaps?

Should I allow my children to see me in bed with my new partner? Even if we're only reading the papers

and wearing glasses, I'm concerned it might cause some long-term Freudian damage.

I'm convinced my daughter would have got better GCSE results if Oscar, her boyfriend, hadn't been on the scene. Annoyingly, Oscar got straight A*s. I want to sue his parents.

An etiquette quandary – my son recently split up with his girlfriend. She left some rather nice pants in his room, which I washed. What is the form here? I would quite like to keep them, as they fit me well.

Everything Else

I've just had my 30-week scan. The baby seems to have a very bulbous nose. I am terrified that this is all I will be able to think when I first see it, and that we won't bond. Why am I so shallow? Aren't I meant to think the scan is the most beautiful thing I've ever seen?

My due date is approaching, and I've become obsessed with my hospital bag. I've been told to pack an extra pillow, a handheld fan, backless slippers, bendy straws, glucose tablets, a birthing ball, distracting magazines and lip balm (gas-and-air is drying). But I'm stuck on what to wear. Should I pack a bikini for the birthing pool, or would that look prudish? Maybe I should just pack the top half, so the baby can get out easily? I haven't even started on the baby's bag.

Is it irresponsible to take my newborn to a toxic-smelling, windowless nail bar? If I don't, my toenails may trigger post-natal depression.

We have ants. And mice. But all pest control methods seem to be lethal to children, too. The only safe option is a 'sonic mouse repellent' – but what if certain children can hear at the same frequency as a mouse, resulting in irrevocable hearing damage?

My son smells of his au pair.
I feel like a jealous wife,
sniffing his scalp for whiffs
of her.

I'm worried that I'm breeding
an anxious child.

My teenage
son has begun
babysitting for
local families.
I encouraged
this, to teach
him the value
of money.
Now I'm
afraid he will

be groomed, and perhaps abducted, by a terrible Mrs Robinson-type mother. He is unusually beautiful.

I can't remember if my daughter works in 'ethical' or 'ethnic' fashion. It's too late to ask. She will accuse me of never listening.

My children have left home,
but they still use our house
as a storage hangar. I keep
accepting more and more stuff,
as I'm afraid that if I don't
they will stop visiting. Could
I draw the line at housing an
enormous trampoline in our
dining room?

Since moving to Hackney, my 24-year-old son has grown a wispy, auburn beard (his head is blond). I fear for his job prospects, but he told me 'everyone in

digital media has a beard'. I can't argue, as I don't know what digital media is. Can I stage a facial hair intervention?

Sometimes I fantasise about taking a very long train journey, alone,

or having
a general
anaesthetic.
Is this normal?

A big thank you to Olivia Guest at Jonathan Clowes, and Katie Cowan, Nicola Newman and Michelle Mac at Pavilion, for making this book possible, and to Denise Dorrance, for her brilliant illustrations and ideas. I'd also like to thank all the mothers who shared their own worries with me, particularly Jane Finlay, Caroline Collett, Nina Rassaby-Lewis, Caireann Conlon, Nina Baruch, Laura Cox-Watson, Anahid Jarvis, Stephanie Morrison, Joanna Mawdsley and Oonagh Blackall. Finally, I am indebted to my mother, Laura, and my son, Finlay.